My sweet and favourite princess,
I will miss you so much, you
always be in my heart and
In my mind.

I love you until the moon
and back

Alba ☆♡

This igloo book belongs to:

.........AMELIE ♥.........................

igloobooks

Published in 2016
by Igloo Books Ltd
Cottage Farm
Sywell
NN6 0BJ
www.igloobooks.com

HUN001 0716
4 6 8 10 9 7 5
ISBN 978-1-78343-306-3

Illustrated by James Newman Gray
Additional illustrations by Nigel Chilvers

Printed and manufactured in China

My Treasury of
Snuggle-Up Stories

Illustrated by
James Newman Gray

igloobooks

Contents

I Love You
This Much

When the weather is cloudy,
if there's just one thing I could do,
it would be to float up in the sky
and bring sunshine home to you.

I'd catch the golden rays in a jar
that glows bright and warm,
to keep you nice and cosy
when there's a scary storm.

To show you how much I love you,
I'd make you a special treat.
It would be the yummiest cake ever,
just for you to eat.

My cake would be big and tall
and covered in lovely, pink cream.
It would be a yummy, scrummy,
sticky, candy-licking dream.

I would do anything to cheer you up
when you're feeling down.
I'd put on a funny show for you
and dress up as a clown.

I'd get my friends to dress up
in a silly circus style,
then I'd wobble on a tightrope,
just to try and make you smile.

I would run through the meadows,
where the wild flowers grow
and pick the best ones for you,
in the soft evening glow.

This special bunch of flowers
would be pink, orange and green,
bursting with lovely blooms
that are the best you've ever seen.

In a magic wood, I'd find out
where the fairies go to hide.
I'd make a wish in the fairy
ring and dance around inside.

6

Fairies would come with their wands and
flutter here and there.
I would make a wish for you to
show you how much I care.

I'd turn into a superhero
and become Super Panda Bear.
If you needed me, I'd zoom up high
and fly through the air.

I'd whoosh over the city,
across the mountains and the sea.
When I finally reach you,
you'd get a super-hug from me.

To show you how much I love you,
I'd climb up a ladder to the sky.
It would reach past clouds and
sunbeams and rainbows way up high.

22

My ladder would stretch up to the
stars and they would shine so bright.
I'd bring the biggest one back for you,
to twinkle through the night.

I'd go up to the mountain top
and shout so everyone could hear.
Then I'd run back down to whisper,
"I love you," in your ear.

I want to tell the world
just how special you are to me,
and that when I'm with you,
I'm as happy as can be.

I love you so much because
I think that you're the very best.
You're all warm and cuddly
and much snugglier than the rest.

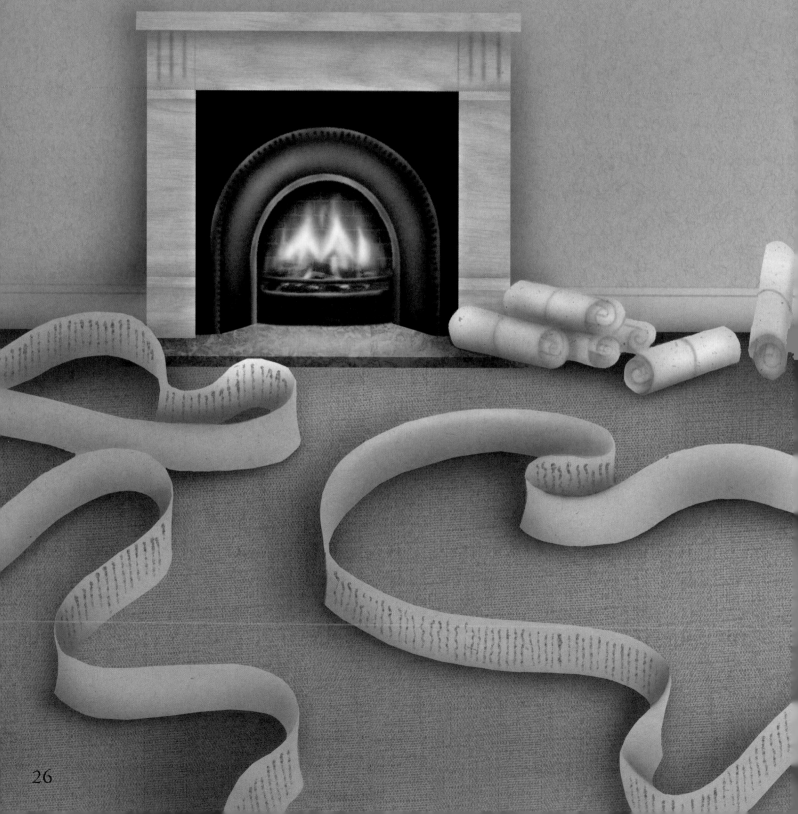

I can think of lots of ways
to tell you how lovely you are,
to let you know what you mean to me
and that you're my shining star.

I'm so lucky that I have you
and you'll always have me, too.
I love you more than anyone,
just because you're you!

New Clothes

Badger couldn't wait to go to the park to play spacemen.
"Wrap up warm," said his dad. Badger tried to wrap up warm,
but his coat was too small, there were holes in his boots
and he could only find one glove!

"Oh dear," laughed Badger's dad. "We'd better go and buy you some new clothes." Badger stomped crossly all the way to the shops. He didn't want new clothes. He wanted to whizz down the big slide and pretend he was shooting into a moon crater.

Suddenly, it started to rain. "We'll have to get the boots first or your feet will get wet," said Badger's dad. They stopped at the shoe shop and bought a pair of shiny, gold boots. "Can we go to the park now, Dad?" asked Badger. "I want to be a spaceman!"

"We need to get you a coat," said Badger's dad. Badger tried on
a shiny, silver coat. "Let's get the matching trousers, too."
They were covered in a pattern of brilliant purple stars.
"Now can we go to the park so I can be a spaceman?" asked Badger.

"You still need some gloves," said Badger's dad. Badger tried
on spotty gloves, fluffy gloves and then, he found a pair of sparkly,
golden gloves. "These ones are perfect," said Badger's dad.
Badger mumbled in agreement. "Please, Dad. Can we go to the
park now?" he asked, running out of the shop.

"Wait," said his dad, smiling. "There's one more thing you need."
In the toyshop, they found a plastic spaceman's helmet.
Badger put it on and looked at himself in the mirror.
"Wow!" shouted Badger, excitedly. "I look just like a spaceman!"

Badger and his dad had finally reached the park.
Badger's friends were already there, swaying on the swings.
Badger jumped towards them like he was walking on the moon.
"You look amazing!" they cried. "Let's pretend the slide is a
rocket ship! The climbing frame can be the moon!"

"Three... two... one... blast-off!" yelled Badger,
as he zoomed down the slide and into outer space.
"Badger looks like a real spaceman," his friends shouted.
I feel like one, too," said Badger. "Thanks for my new clothes, Dad."

The Magic Toy Box

The clock struck twelve at Lucy's house
and all were fast asleep.
Across the moonlit bedroom floor,
shadows began to creep.

40

A sound came from the toy box.
The lid creaked and opened wide.
"It's time to play," whispered Teddy,
to all the toys inside.

The disco lights, shining bright,
swirled and whirled around.

"Nearly ready," Teddy said,
"Now we need some sound!"

Hippo wiggled and Monkey giggled,
as all the toys began to bop.

Singing along, as he danced to the song,
Bunny went hippety-hop!

"Time for a break!" cried Teddy,
as his hungry tummy rumbled.
Into the kitchen, to find some treats,
the happy toys all tumbled.

They piled their plates with cookies and cake
and tasty things to eat.
Monkey munched, Croc went crunch
and they gobbled up every sweet.

At last the toys were really full
and couldn't eat one bite more.
It was time to tidy up.
Bunny started sweeping the floor.

Washing the dishes,
scrub, scrub, scrub,
Teddy made a splash.
Drying them off, rub-a-dub-dub,
Puppy finished in a flash.

53

Outside the stars were fading fast
and it was nearly dawn.
"Back to the toy box everyone,"
said Teddy, with a yawn.

Up the stairs, the toys all climbed,
as quickly as they could go.
Teddy felt very sleepy,
his little legs started to slow.

55

"Hurry!" whispered Bunny,
as he hopped up into the chest.

"Hey! Wait for me!" cried Teddy,
who had stopped to take a rest.

56

The toy box lid was closing,
so Teddy laid on the floor.

Soon, he was in a deep sleep
and softly began to snore.

When morning came, Lucy woke up
and shook her sleepy head.
She saw the sunshine streaming in
and jumped out of her bed.

Looking around her bedroom,
Lucy blinked and rubbed her eyes.
How did my bear get over **there?**
She thought, to her surprise.

"Lovely Bear," said Lucy,
as she kissed and cuddled him tight.
"I wonder what you were doing,
while I was asleep last night."

One night, when the room went dark,
Baby Bear began to feel frightened.

"Please leave the light on," he called.
"I'm scared of the dark!"

"Don't be afraid," said Mummy, taking Baby Bear's
hand and leading him to the window.
"Not everything about night-time is dark.
Look outside and see how magical it can be."

Through the window,
Baby Bear could see
that the sky was
filled with bright,
shining stars.
"Why don't you make
a wish?" said Mummy.
"I wish I wasn't so
afraid of the dark,"
whispered Baby Bear.

As he spoke, one
little star began to
shimmer and shake.
Then, suddenly,
it shot across
the sky in a shower
of sparkles. The bears
watched in amazement
as it flew past the
window and landed
in their garden.

"Quick!" called Mummy, racing downstairs to see the star.

"Wait for me!" cried Baby Bear, grabbing his teddy and following behind.

"Look," whispered Mummy, opening the door.
Baby Bear gasped. He could see the star
glowing in the darkness.
"Let's go and see if we can find it," said Mummy.

Mummy stepped outside and Baby Bear peeked out from behind her. The garden seemed huge and dark and scary.

Th

Something flew over their heads and hooted
with a loud, "Twit-twoo!"
"I don't like it," said Baby Bear.
"I don't want to go out there!"

"Those are fireflies," replied Mummy. "They light up at night."
"Wow!" said Baby Bear. "They're not scary
at all. Are there other animals that
come out at night?"

"Yes, look over there," said Mummy, pointing.
"Those bunnies are playing together in the moonlight."
"That looks like fun," said Baby Bear, giggling.

Further along the path, Baby Bear heard the
hooting sound that had frightened him before. "Twit-twoo!"
"What's that?" he cried, hiding behind Mummy.

"It's just an owl," said Mummy, smiling.
"Hello, Owl," said Baby Bear. "We're looking for a fallen star.
Have you seen it?" The owl hooted again
and Baby Bear laughed.

Baby Bear could see that the shimmery light of the star
wasn't far away. He was so excited he couldn't wait to see it.
"Come on, Mummy," he said. "We're almost there!"

The bears hurried ahead until they finally spotted
the star lying in the grass. It glittered and glowed brightly.
Little bunnies hopped around it, wondering what it was.

Back in bed, Baby Bear tucked the star
under his pillow to keep it safe.
"Goodnight, Baby Bear," said Mummy.
"Goodnight, Mummy," replied Baby Bear.

This time, when Mummy turned out the light,
Baby Bear wasn't scared at all. His special star sparkled
in the darkness, as he snuggled up, sleepily.

Baby Bear fell asleep, dreaming of all the wonderful
things he had seen on his adventure. After that night,
he was never afraid of the dark again.

Let's Make Believe

"Let's not build a snowman," Little Bear said.
"I've got a much better plan instead!
We'll make a snow spaceship and travel to Mars.
Let's zoom round the moon and then visit the stars."

"Let's play snow pirates!" Little Bear roared.
"We'll go on a snow ship with treasure aboard.
We won't mind if the weather is icy and cold,
As long as we have all our huge bags of gold."

"Let's make a snow castle!" Little Bear cried.
"We'll have turrets and thrones and a moat that is wide.
We'll be kings and queens for the whole of the day.
People will have to do whatever we say!"

"Let's be snow explorers," Little Bear smiled.
"We can search for ice monsters that live in the wild.
We'll look for their footprints and track them and then,
Tomorrow we'll do it all over again."

Starlight Wishes

When the silvery moon shines
and we should be tucked up snug in bed,
we sit by our window
and dream of magic adventures instead.

We watch for an enchanted star,
shooting through the sky with a swish.
We'd imagine what we could do
if it granted our every wish.

Feeling so small, on a mountain so tall,
covered in sparkly snow,
We'd find a sled, all shiny and red
and shout, "Ready… steady… Go!"

Cold from our noses down to our toes,
we'd whoosh through the frosty air.
Faster and faster we'd swoosh and slide,
swirling snowflakes in the air.

On a faraway desert island,
we'd be pirates brave and bold.
Wearing sailors' hats and a black eyepatch,
we'd dig deep for buried gold.

In the soft sand we'd find
an old treasure chest bursting at the seams,
Filled to the brim with precious gems
and jewels beyond our wildest dreams.

We'd ride round the world
on a rollercoaster,
crying out,
"Whoopee!"

With great big swoops

and loop the loops,

we'd speed over
the land and sea.

104

We'd whoosh up high,
right up to the sky.

Up and up we'd climb.

Zoooom!

We'd zoom down
fast with our
hands in the air,
then do it one
more time!

We'd slide down a sparkling rainbow
of orange and ruby red, too.
Sherbety yellow and gumdrop green
and beautiful, bright sky blue.

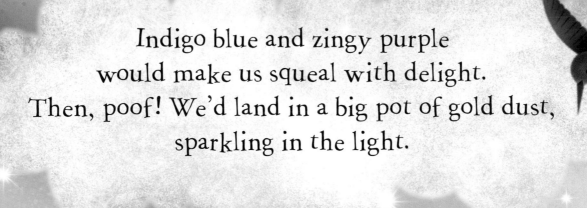

Indigo blue and zingy purple
would make us squeal with delight.
Then, poof! We'd land in a big pot of gold dust,
sparkling in the light.

On candyfloss clouds we'd float
to a land where everything is sweet.
Marshmallow mountains and lollipop trees,
ready for us to eat!

There'd be houses made of gingerbread
and cakes filled with fluffy cream.
We'd gobble up all the tasty treats,
like the most delicious dream.

We'd fly to a land where stories come true,
in an enchanted wood.
Meeting Goldilocks, Cinderella
and Little Red Riding Hood.

Rapunzel would climb from her tower.
Beauty would wake in her bed.
We'd make lots of fairy tale friends
from the bedtime stories we'd read.

We'd zoom to the moon on our cosy beds
and see the earth below.
The stars would twinkle diamond bright
and the planets would softly glow.

Floating through the quiet blue,
we'd collect stars as we glided by.
Then, down and down we'd slowly drift,
through the deep, starry midnight sky.

114

Soon we'd be safely back at home,
in the very best place of all.

In our snuggly little bedroom,
we'd hang our stars up on the wall.

Starlight would shine all around
and remind us that wishes come true.
They whisk us to magical places
with lots of fun things to do.

117

Rainy Day Treasure

Chipmunk was spending a rainy day at Grandma's house.
It was too wet to play outside, so Grandma said, "Let's have
a treasure hunt!" Grandma read the first clue aloud.
"TO FIND A CLUE, LOOK IN A SHOE."

Chipmunk scampered into the hall and started to search.
She tipped up big shoes and little shoes, rubber boots and
fluffy slippers. A piece of paper fluttered to the ground and
she scooped it up. It was the next clue!

"WHO'S IN THE BATH? TRY NOT TO LAUGH," read Chipmunk.
She raced upstairs to the bathroom.
Two funny, plastic ducks were sitting in the bathtub.
Chipmunk giggled as she pulled a piece of paper
out of one of the ducks' beaks.

"I'M UNDER YOUR HEAD, WHEN YOU'RE IN BED,"
she said aloud. Chipmunk scrambled onto Grandma's bed.
Boing! It was very bouncy.
Grandma's frilly pillows fell on the floor
and Chipmunk saw the next clue.

"LOOK IN A TRUNK, LITTLE CHIPMUNK," read Chipmunk.
She rushed to the attic and searched through a trunk
full of old clothes. She found a big, flowery hat and tried it on.
The clue fell out onto her nose!

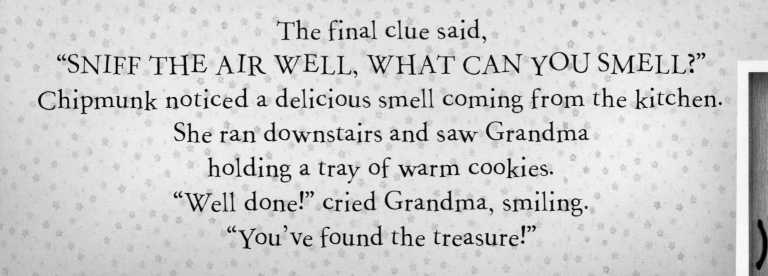

The final clue said,
"SNIFF THE AIR WELL, WHAT CAN YOU SMELL?"
Chipmunk noticed a delicious smell coming from the kitchen.
She ran downstairs and saw Grandma
holding a tray of warm cookies.
"Well done!" cried Grandma, smiling.
"You've found the treasure!"

Jungle
Parade

On a hot, lazy day in the deep,
deep jungle, the animals were snoozing
in the afternoon sun.

128

All except Little Elephant,
who swished his trunk
this way and that,
this way and that.

Swish,
swish!

129

"What's that hissing and swishing?"
asked the parrots in the treetops.
They fluffed up their feathers
and they all went **squawk**!

In the branches of the trees,
the monkeys stopped snoozing.
They listened to the **swishing**
and the **hissing** and
Parrot going **squawk!**

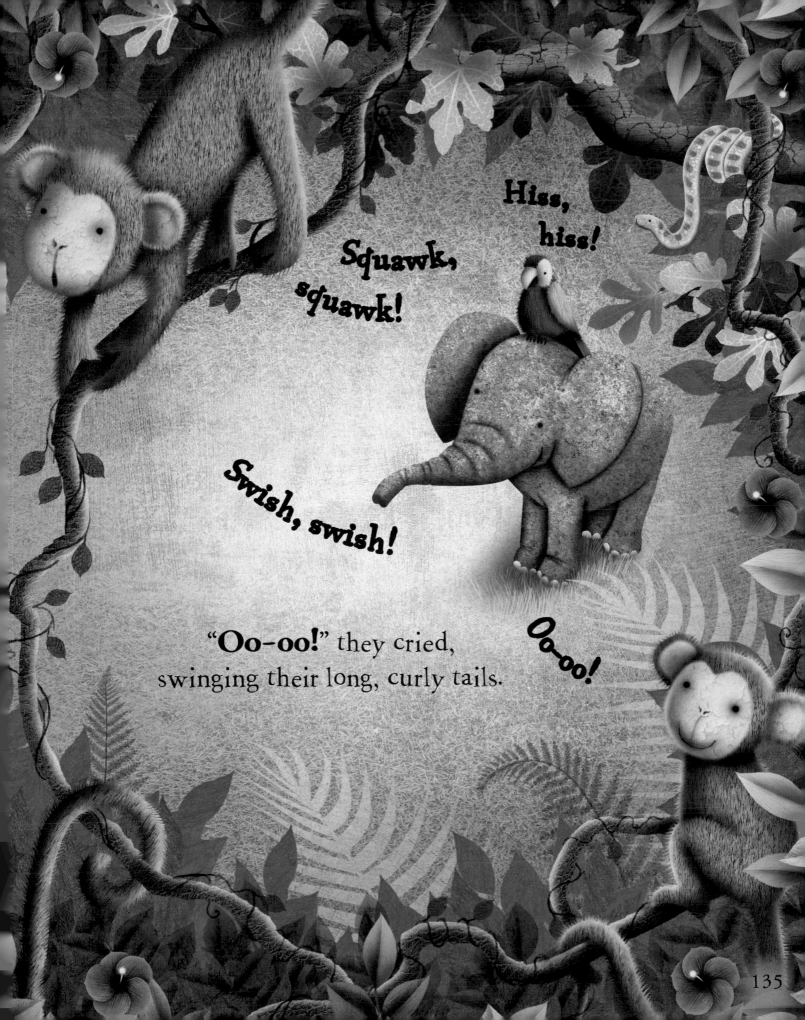

Squawk, squawk!

Hiss, hiss!

Swish, swish!

"Oo-oo!" they cried, swinging their long, curly tails.

Oo-oo!

In the cool waterhole, the big hippos went **glug**,
blowing bubbles as they bathed.

Glug, glug, went Hippo
and he joined the jungle parade.

136

Along the riverbank, the animals came
with a **swish** and a **hiss**
and a very loud **squawk**,
an **oo-oo** and a **glug, glug**.
"What fun!" thought Crocodile
and gave a very loud **SNAP!**

Oo-oo!

Glug, glug!

139

Those jungle animals made so much noise
as they passed by Lion's quiet, cool cave.

140

ROAR!

Swish,
swish!

Sleepy Lion leapt out and gave a great big **ROAR!**
Then everyone stopped and there wasn't a sound.

Then, from the jungle came a rustle
and a bustle and a rumble and a thunder.
The trees shook and the ground shook
and there was a very loud **TRUMPET!**

It was Little Elephant's
mummy and daddy.

143

"Where were you?" asked Daddy Elephant, flapping his ears.
"With all my new friends," replied Little Elephant.
"We're having a jungle parade!"

Snake went **hiss** and Parrot gave a **squawk**.
Oo-oo went Monkey and Hippo went **glug**.
Snap went Crocodile and **ROAR** went Lion.

The moon came out and little stars sparkled.
Not a sound could be heard in the hush of the night,
not even the swish of Little Elephant's trunk.
He was fast asleep.

Winter Knitting

Fox's mummy loves to knit. She curls up in her chair.
She makes socks and scarves and hats for little Fox to wear.

Sometimes the socks come out too big and the hats come out too tight.
Sometimes the scarves are just too long. It's hard to get it right.

Most of them fit perfectly and then his mum is done.
Then, Fox is snuggly and warm and ready for wintry fun.

When the garden fills with snow, Fox runs to play out there.
All the clothes that don't fit him, his snowman loves to wear!

Night-time Bunny

Deep in the wood, in a snuggly burrow,
hungry Bunny was having his supper.
It was nearly bedtime and he was slurping
the last of his delicious carrot soup.

"Mummy, do all the animals in the wood go to bed when it gets dark?" asked Bunny. "No," said Mummy, "some of them sleep during the day and wake up at night."

Bunny thought being awake at night sounded very exciting. "Please can I see the animals that come out at night?" he asked. "I want to be a night-time bunny!"

Mummy's knitting needles clicked and clacked.
"Okay," she said, putting her knitting down,
"let's go for a walk together to see
the night-time animals."

Bunny couldn't wait to
go on his night-time adventure
and he bounced out of the burrow.
Outside, the sunset sky
was orange and pink.

"It's so beautiful,"
said Bunny.

160

"Keep close," Mummy said,
as she closed the front door.
"We need to stick together."

Bunny hopped close to Mummy for a while,
but then, he spotted something strange.
With a hoppety-hop, he went
over to investigate.

There, lying among the flowers,
was a strange ball of prickles.
Bunny crouched down
and sniffed the prickly thing.

Suddenly, it uncurled.
A face and four paws popped out
and a little voice squeaked,
"Hello, I'm Hedgehog."

The hedgehog began to roly-poly around on the ground and Bunny joined in. "This is fun!" he giggled.

Then, Bunny rolled into Hedgehog and pricked his paw on the prickles. "Ouch, that hurt!" cried Bunny.

Mummy rubbed Bunny's paw.
"Never mind," she said, leading Bunny along the
woodland path. Soon, they came to a little pond
where sleeping ducks tucked
their beaks under their wings.

The night was full of strange noises.
There were hoots and flutters and screeches and barks.
"What are those noises?" asked Bunny, nervously.
"They're night animals," replied Mummy,
"they're nothing to be afraid of."

Suddenly, a great, dark shape
swooped past Bunny. It was big
and feathery and made strange noises.
SWOOSH! Twit-twoo!

Little Bunny dived
into a patch of grass.
"Mummy, it's a monster!" he cried.

"Don't worry, Bunny."
said Mummy.
"It's just the night owl.
He won't hurt you."

167

Bunny wasn't listening to Mummy.
He ran, hoppety-hoppety-hop
along the shadowy woodland path.
Suddenly, something black and white
and furry came out of a hole.

THUMP! Bunny bumped straight into it.
"OUCH!" cried a very grumpy badger.
"Watch where you're going!"

Bunny rubbed his sore nose. His little ears drooped and he
felt sad. The night-time animals didn't seem friendly at all.

Just then, little fluttery bats flew past.
Bunny thought they looked very funny.
They whizzed between his ears
and round his fluffy, white tail.
Bunny giggled and chased them
round and round.

"Where are you, Mummy?" called Bunny from the wood.

Bunny felt so dizzy, he didn't know which way was up.

He tried to hop, but he wibbled and wobbled until he fell, thump, right on his bottom.

171

Then, between the trees,
there was a flash of orange.
Something stepped out
into the moonlight.
It was a big, red,
bushy-tailed fox.

"Well, if it isn't a little bunny,"
said the sly fox, grinning.
"What are YOU doing out all
alone at this time of night?"

Suddenly, Mummy hopped
out from the trees. "He's being
a night-time bunny!" she cried.
The frightened fox leapt off into
the wood and Mummy
and Bunny were alone again.

"You mustn't run off
like that again, Bunny,"
said Mummy.

"Can we go home now?"
asked Bunny, sleepily.
"I'm tired and I want to go to bed."

"Okay," said Mummy,
giving him a cuddle.

"Let's go home then,"
she said. "I'll tuck you up so
you're snuggly and warm."

In his cosy, bunny bed,
inside the snuggly, bunny burrow,
Bunny thought about everything
he'd seen in the woods that night.

He yawned a little and pulled his blanket up to his chin,
"I think I prefer being a daytime bunny," he said.
Mummy smiled, kissed him on the forehead and turned
off his bedside light, "Sweet dreams, my little bunny."